The Countess Cathleen

W. B. Yeats

ISBN: 1977527515

ISBN-13: 978-1977527516

Table of Contents

SCENE—A room with lighted fire, and a door into the open air, through which one sees, perhaps, the trees of a wood, and these trees should be painted in flat colour upon a gold or diapered sky. The walls are of one colour. The scene should have the effect of missal Painting. MARY, a woman of forty years or so, is grinding a quern.

MARY. What can have made the grey hen flutter so?

(TEIG, a boy of fourteen, is coming in with turf, which he lays beside the hearth.)

TEIG. They say that now the land is famine struck The graves are walking.

MARY. There is something that the hen hears.

TEIG. And that is not the worst; at Tubber-vanach A woman met a man with ears spread out, And they moved up and down like a bat's wing.

MARY. What can have kept your father all this while?

TEIG. Two nights ago, at Carrick-orus churchyard, A herdsman met a man who had no mouth, Nor eyes, nor ears; his face a wall of flesh; He saw him plainly by the light of the moon.

MARY. Look out, and tell me if your father's coming.

(TEIG goes to door.)

TEIG. Mother!

MARY. What is it?

TEIG. In the bush beyond, There are two birds—if you can call them birds— I could not see them rightly for the leaves. But they've the shape and colour of horned owls And I'm half certain they've a human face.

MARY. Mother of God, defend us!

TEIG. They're looking at me. What is the good of praying? father says. God and the Mother of God have dropped asleep. What do they care, he says, though the whole land Squeal like a rabbit under a weasel's tooth?

MARY. You'll bring misfortune with your blasphemies Upon your father, or yourself, or me. I would to God he were home—ah, there he is.

(SHEMUS comes in.)

What was it kept you in the wood? You know I cannot get all sorts of accidents Out of my mind till you are home again.

SHEMUS. I'm in no mood to listen to your clatter. Although I tramped the woods for half a day, I've taken nothing, for the very rats, Badgers, and hedgehogs seem to have died of drought, And there was scarce a wind in the parched leaves.

TEIG. Then you have brought no dinner.

SHEMUS. After that I sat among the beggars at the cross-roads, And held a hollow hand among the others.

MARY. What, did you beg?

SHEMUS. I had no chance to beg, For when the beggars saw me they cried out They would not have another share their alms, And hunted me away with sticks and stones.

TEIG. You said that you would bring us food or money.

SHEMUS. What's in the house?

TEIG. A bit of mouldy bread.

MARY. There's flour enough to make another loaf.

TEIG. And when that's gone?

MARY. There is the hen in the coop.

SHEMUS. My curse upon the beggars, my Curse upon them!

TEIG. And the last penny gone.

SHEMUS. When the hen's gone, What can we do but live on sorrel and dock) And dandelion, till our mouths are green?

MARY. God, that to this hour's found bit and sup, Will cater for us still.

SHEMUS. His kitchen's bare. There were five doors that I looked through this day And saw the dead and not a soul to wake them.

MARY. Maybe He'd have us die because He knows, When the ear is stopped and when the eye is stopped, That every wicked sight is hid from the eye, And all fool talk from the ear.

SHEMUS. Who's passing there? And mocking us with music?

(A stringed instrument without.)

TEIG. A young man plays it, There's an old woman and a lady with him.

SHEMUS. What is the trouble of the poor to her? Nothing at all or a harsh radishy sauce For the day's meat.

MARY. God's pity on the rich, Had we been through as many doors, and seen The dishes standing on the polished wood In the wax candle light, we'd be as hard, And there's the needle's eye at the end of all.

SHEMUS. My curse upon the rich.

TEIG. They're coming here.

SHEMUS. Then down upon that stool, down quick, I say, And call up a whey face and a whining voice, And let your head be bowed upon your knees.

MARY. Had I but time to put the place to rights.

(CATHLEEN, OONA, and ALEEL enter.)

CATHLEEN. God save all here. There is a certain house, An old grey castle with a kitchen garden, A cider orchard and a plot for flowers, Somewhere among these woods.

MARY. We know it, lady. A place that's set among impassable walls As though world's trouble could not find it out.

CATHLEEN. It may be that we are that trouble, for we— Although we've wandered in the wood this hour— Have lost it too, yet I should know my way, For I lived all my childhood in that house.

MARY. Then you are Countess Cathleen?

CATHLEEN. And this woman, Oona, my nurse, should have remembered it, For we were happy for a long time there.

OONA. The paths are overgrown with thickets now, Or else some change has come upon my sight.

CATHLEEN. And this young man, that should have known the woods— Because we met him on their border but now, Wandering and singing like a wave of the sea— Is so wrapped up in dreams of terrors to come That he can give no help.

MARY. You have still some way, But I can put you on the trodden path Your servants take when they are marketing. But first sit down and rest yourself awhile, For my old fathers served your fathers, lady, Longer than books can tell—and it were strange If you and yours should not be welcome here.

CATHLEEN. And it were stranger still were I ungrateful For such kind welcome but I must be gone, For the night's gathering in.

SHEMUS. It is a long while Since I've set eyes on bread or on what buys it.

CATHLEEN. So you are starving even in this wood, Where I had thought I would find nothing changed. But that's a dream, for the old worm o' the world Can eat its way into what place it pleases.

(She gives money.)

TEIG. Beautiful lady, give me something too; I fell but now, being weak with hunger and thirst, And lay upon the threshold like a log.

CATHLEEN. I gave for all and that was all I had. Look, my purse is empty. I have passed By starving men and women all this day, And they have had the rest; but take the purse, The silver clasps on't may be worth a trifle. But if you'll come to-morrow to my house You shall have twice the sum.

(ALEEL begins to play.)

SHEMUS (muttering). What, music, music!

CATHLEEN. Ah, do not blame the finger on the string; The doctors bid me fly the unlucky times And find distraction for my thoughts, or else Pine to my grave.

SHEMUS. I have said nothing, lady. Why should the like of us complain?

OONA. Have done. Sorrows that she's but read of in a book Weigh on her mind as if they had been her own.

(OONA, MARY, and CATHLEEN go Out. ALEEL looks defiantly at SHEMUS.)

ALEEL. (Singing) Impetuous heart, be still, be still, Your sorrowful love can never be told, Cover it up with a lonely tune, He that could bend all things to His will Has covered the door of the infinite fold With the pale stars and the wandering moon.

(He takes a step towards the door and then turns again.)

Shut to the door before the night has fallen, For who can say what walks, or in what shape Some devilish creature flies in the air, but now Two grey-horned owls hooted above our heads.

(He goes out, his singing dies away. MARY comes in. SHEmus has been counting the money.)

TEIG. There's no good luck in owls, but it may be That the ill luck's to fall upon their heads.

MARY. You never thanked her ladyship.

SHEMUS. Thank her, For seven halfpence and a silver bit?

TEIG. But for this empty purse?

8

SHEMUS. What's that for thanks, Or what's the double of it that she promised? With bread and flesh and every sort of food Up to a price no man has heard the like of And rising every day.

MARY. We have all she had; She emptied out the purse before our eyes.

SHEMUS (to MARY, who has gone to close the door) Leave that door open.

MARY. When those that have read books, And seen the seven wonders of the world, Fear what's above or what's below the ground, It's time that poverty should bolt the door.

SHEMUS. I'll have no bolts, for there is not a thing That walks above the ground or under it I had not rather welcome to this house Than any more of mankind, rich or poor.

TEIG. So that they brought us money.

SHEMUS. I heard say There's something that appears like a white bird, A pigeon or a seagull or the like, But if you hit it with a stone or a stick It clangs as though it had been made of brass; And that if you dig down where it was scratching You'll find a crock of gold.

TEIG. But dream of gold For three nights running, and there's always gold.

SHEMUS. You might be starved before you've dug it out.

TEIG. But maybe if you called, something would come, They have been seen of late.

MARY. Is it call devils? Call devils from the wood, call them in here?

SHEMUS. So you'd stand up against me, and you'd say Who or what I am to welcome here.

9

(He hits her.)

That is to show who's master.

TEIG. Call them in.

MARY. God help us all!

SHEMUS. Pray, if you have a mind to. it's little that the sleepy ears above Care for your words; but I'll call what I please.

TEIG. There is many a one, they say, had money from them.

SHEMUS. (at door) Whatever you are that walk the woods at night, So be it that you have not shouldered up Out of a grave—for I'll have nothing human— And have free hands, a friendly trick of speech, I welcome you. Come, sit beside the fire. What matter if your head's below your arms Or you've a horse's tail to whip your flank, Feathers instead of hair, that's but a straw, Come, share what bread and meat is in the house, And stretch your heels and warm them in the ashes. And after that, let's share and share alike And curse all men and women. Come in, come in. What, is there no one there?

(Turning from door)

And yet they say They are as common as the grass, and ride Even upon the book in the priest's hand.

(TEIG lifts one arm slowly and points toward the door and begins moving backwards. SHEMUS turns, he also sees something and begins moving backward. MARY does the same. A man dressed as an Eastern merchant comes in carrying a small carpet. He unrolls it and sits cross-legged at one end of it. Another man dressed in the same way follows, and sits at the other end. This is done slowly and deliberately. When they are seated they take money out of embroidered purses at their girdles and begin arranging it on the carpet.

TEIG. You speak to them.

SHEMUS. No, you.

TEIG. 'Twas you that called them.

SHEMUS. (coming nearer) I'd make so bold, if you would pardon it, To ask if there's a thing you'd have of us. Although we are but poor people, if there is, Why, if there is—

FIRST MERCHANT. We've travelled a long road, For we are merchants that must tramp the world, And now we look for supper and a fire And a safe corner to count money in.

SHEMUS. I thought you were.... but that's no matter now— There had been words between my wife and me Because I said I would be master here, And ask in what I pleased or who I pleased And so.... but that is nothing to the point, Because it's certain that you are but merchants.

FIRST MERCHANT. We travel for the Master of all merchants.

SHEMUS. Yet if you were that I had thought but now I'd welcome you no less. Be what you please And you'll have supper at the market rate, That means that what was sold for but a penny Is now worth fifty.

(MERCHANTS begin putting money on carpet.)

FIRST MERCHANT. Our Master bids us pay So good a price, that all who deal with us Shall eat, drink, and be merry.

SHEMUS. (to MARY) Bestir yourself, Go kill and draw the fowl, while Teig and I Lay out the plates and make a better fire.

MARY. I will not cook for you.

SHEMUS. Not cook! not cook! Do not be angry. She wants to pay me back Because I struck her in that argument. But she'll get sense again. Since the dearth came We rattle one on another as though we were Knives thrown into a basket to be cleaned.

MARY. I will not cook for you, because I know In what unlucky shape you sat but now Outside this door.

TEIG. It's this, your honours: Because of some wild words my father said She thinks you are not of those who cast a shadow.

SHEMUS. I said I'd make the devils of the wood Welcome, if they'd a mind to eat and drink; But it is certain that you are men like us.

FIRST MERCHANT. It's strange that she should think we cast no shadow, For there is nothing on the ridge of the world That's more substantial than the merchants are That buy and sell you.

MARY. If you are not demons, And seeing what great wealth is spread out there, Give food or money to the starving poor.

FIRST MERCHANT. If we knew how to find deserving poor We'd do our share.

MARY. But seek them patiently.

FIRST MERCHANT. We know the evils of mere charity.

MARY. Those scruples may befit a common time. I had thought there was a pushing to and fro, At times like this, that overset the scale And trampled measure down.

FIRST MERCHANT. But if already We'd thought of a more prudent way than that?

SECOND MERCHANT. If each one brings a bit of merchandise, We'll give him such a price he never dreamt of.

MARY. Where shall the starving come at merchandise?

FIRST MERCHANT. We will ask nothing but what all men have.

MARY. Their swine and cattle, fields and implements Are sold and gone.

FIRST MERCHANT. They have not sold all yet. For there's a vaporous thing—that may be nothing, But that's the buyer's risk—a second self, They call immortal for a story's sake.

SHEMUS. You come to buy our souls?

TEIG. I'll barter mine. Why should we starve for what may be but nothing?

MARY. Teig and Shemus—

SHEMUS. What can it be but nothing? What has God poured out of His bag but famine? Satan gives money.

TEIG. Yet no thunder stirs.

FIRST MERCHANT. There is a heap for each.

(SHEMUS goes to take money.)

But no, not yet, For there's a work I have to set you to.

SHEMUS. So then you're as deceitful as the rest, And all that talk of buying what's but a vapour Is fancy bred. I might have known as much, Because that's how the trick-o'-the-loop man talks.

FIRST MERCHANT. That's for the work, each has its separate price; But neither price is paid till the work's done.

TEIG. The same for me.

MARY. Oh, God, why are you still?

FIRST MERCHANT. You've but to cry aloud at every cross-road, At every house door, that we buy men's souls, And give so good a price that all may live In mirth and comfort till the famine's done, Because we are Christian men.

SHEMUS. Come, let's away.

TREIG> I shall keep running till I've earned the price.

SECOND MERCHANT. (who has risen and gone towards fire) Stop, for we obey a generous Master, That would be served by Comfortable men. And here's your entertainment on the road.

(TRIG and SHEMUS have stopped. TEIG takes the money. They go out.)

MARY. Destroyers of souls, God will destroy you quickly. You shall at last dry like dry leaves and hang Nailed like dead vermin to the doors of God.

SECOND MERCHANT. Curse to your fill, for saints will have their dreams.

FIRST MERCHANTm Though we're but vermin that our Master sent To overrun the world, he at the end Shall pull apart the pale ribs of the moon And quench the stars in the ancestral night.

MARY. God is all powerful.

SECOND MERCHANT. Pray, you shall need Him. You shall eat dock and grass, and dandelion, Till that low threshold there becomes a wall, And when your hands can scarcely drag your body We shall be near you.

(MARY faints.) (The FIRST MERCHANT takes up the carPet, spreads it before the fire and stands in front of it warming his hands.)

FIRST MERCHANT. Our faces go unscratched, For she has fainted. Wring the neck o' that fowl, Scatter the flour and search the shelves for bread. We'll turn the fowl upon the spit and roast it, And eat the supper we were bidden to, Now that the house is quiet, praise our master, And stretch and warm our heels among the ashes.

END OF SCENE 1

SCENE 2

FRONT SCENE.—A wood with perhaps distant view of turreted house at one side, but all in flat colour, without light and shade and against a diafiered or gold background.

COUNTESS CATHLEEN comes in leaning Upon ALEEL's arm. OONA follows them.

CATHLEEN. (Stopping) Surely this leafy corner, where one smells The wild bee's honey, has a story too?

OONA. There is the house at last.

ALEEL. A man, they say, Loved Maeve the Queen of all the invisible host, And died of his love nine centuries ago. And now, when the moon's riding at the full, She leaves her dancers lonely and lies there Upon that level place, and for three days Stretches and sighs and wets her long pale cheeks.

CATHLEEN. So she loves truly.

15

ALEEL. No, but wets her cheeks, Lady, because she has forgot his name.

CATHLEEN. She'd sleep that trouble away—though it must be A heavy trouble to forget his name— If she had better sense.

OONA. Your own house, lady.

ALEEL. She sleeps high up on wintry Knock-na-rea In an old cairn of stones; while her poor women Must lie and jog in the wave if they would sleep Being water born—yet if she cry their names They run up on the land and dance in the moon Till they are giddy and would love as men do, And be as patient and as pitiful. But there is nothing that will stop in their heads, They've such poor memories, though they weep for it. Oh, yes, they weep; that's when the moon is full.

CATHLEEN. is it because they have short memories They live so long?

ALEEL. What's memory but the ash That chokes our fires that have begun to sink? And they've a dizzy, everlasting fire.

OONA. There is your own house, lady.

CATHLEEN. Why, that's true, And we'd have passed it without noticing.

ALEEL. A curse upon it for a meddlesome house! Had it but stayed away I would have known What Queen Maeve thinks on when the moon is pinched; And whether now—as in the old days—the dancers Set their brief love on men.

OONA. Rest on my arm. These are no thoughts for any Christian ear.

ALEEL. I am younger, she would be too heavy for you.

(He begins taking his lute out of the bag, CATHLEEN, Who has turned towards OONA, turns back to him.)

This hollow box remembers every foot That danced upon the level grass of the world, And will tell secrets if I whisper to it. (Sings.) Lift up the white knee; That's what they sing, Those young dancers That in a ring Raved but now Of the hearts that break Long, long ago For their sake.

OONA. New friends are sweet.

ALEEL. "But the dance changes.

Lift up the gown, All that sorrow Is trodden down."

OONA. The empty rattle-pate! Lean on this arm, That I can tell you is a christened arm, And not like some, if we are to judge by speech. But as you please. It is time I was forgot. Maybe it is not on this arm you slumbered When you were as helpless as a worm.

ALEEL. Stay with me till we come to your own house.

CATHLEEN (Sitting down) When I am rested I will need no help.

ALEEL. I thought to have kept her from remembering

The evil of the times for full ten minutes; But now when seven are out you come between.

OONA. Talk on; what does it matter what you say, For you have not been christened?

ALEEL. Old woman, old woman, You robbed her of three minutes peace of mind, And though you live unto a hundred years, And wash the feet of beggars and give alms, And climb Croaghpatrick, you shall not be pardoned.

OONA. How does a man who never was baptized Know what Heaven pardons?

ALEEL. You are a sinful woman

OONA. I care no more than if a pig had grunted.

(Enter CATHLEEN's Steward.)

STEWARD. I am not to blame, for I had locked the gate, The forester's to blame. The men climbed in At the east corner where the elm-tree is.

CATHLEEN. I do not understand you, who has climbed?

STEWARD. Then God be thanked, I am the first to tell you. I was afraid some other of the servants— Though I've been on the watch—had been the first And mixed up truth and lies, your ladyship.

CATHLEEN (rising) Has some misfortune happened?

STEWARD. Yes, indeed. The forester that let the branches lie Against the wall's to blame for everything, For that is how the rogues got into the garden.

CATHLEEN. I thought to have escaped misfortune here. Has any one been killed?

STEWARD. Oh, no, not killed. They have stolen half a cart-load of green cabbage.

CATHLEEN. But maybe they were starving.

STEWARD. That is certain. To rob or starve, that was the choice they had.

CATHLEEN. A learned theologian has laid down That starving men may take what's necessary, And yet be sinless.

OONA. Sinless and a thief There should be broken bottles on the wall.

CATHLEEN. And if it be a sin, while faith's unbroken God cannot help but pardon. There is no soul But it's unlike all others in the world, Nor one but lifts a strangeness to God's love Till that's grown infinite, and therefore none Whose loss were less than irremediable Although it were the wickedest in the world.

(Enter TEIG and SHEMUS.)

STEWARD. What are you running for? Pull off your cap, Do you not see who's there?

SHEMUS. I cannot wait. I am running to the world with the best news That has been brought it for a thousand years.

STEWARD. Then get your breath and speak.

SHEMUS. If you'd my news You'd run as fast and be as out of breath.

TEIG. Such news, we shall be carried on men's shoulders.

SHEMUS. There's something every man has carried with him And thought no more about than if it were A mouthful of the wind; and now it's grown A marketable thing!

TEIG. And yet it seemed As useless as the paring of one's nails.

SHEMUS. What sets me laughing when I think of it, Is that a rogue who's lain in lousy straw, If he but sell it, may set up his coach.

TEIG. (laughing) There are two gentlemen who buy men's souls.

19

CATHLEEN. O God!

TEIG. And maybe there's no soul at all.

STEWARD. They're drunk or mad.

TEIG. Look at the price they give. (Showing money.)

SHEMUS. (tossing up money) "Go cry it all about the world," they said. "Money for souls, good money for a soul."

CATHLEEN. Give twice and thrice and twenty times their money, And get your souls again. I will pay all.

SHEMUS. Not we! not we! For souls—if there are souls— But keep the flesh out of its merriment. I shall be drunk and merry.

TEIG. Come, let's away.

(He goes.)

CATHLEEN. But there's a world to come.

SHEMUS. And if there is, I'd rather trust myself into the hands That can pay money down than to the hands That have but shaken famine from the bag.

(He goes Out R.)

(lilting) "There's money for a soul, sweet yellow money. There's money for men's souls, good money, money."

CATHLEEN. (to ALEEL) Go call them here again, bring them by force, Beseech them, bribe, do anything you like.

(ALEEL goes.)

And you too follow, add your prayers to his.

20

(OONA, who has been praying, goes out.)

Steward, you know the secrets of my house. How much have I?

STEWARD. A hundred kegs of gold.

CATHLEEN. How much have I in castles?

STEWARD. As much more.

CATHLEEN. How much have I in pasture?

STEWARD. As much more.

CATHLEEN. How much have I in forests?

STEWARD. As much more.

CATHLEEN. Keeping this house alone, sell all I have, Go barter where you please, but come again With herds of cattle and with ships of meal.

STEWARD. God's blessing light upon your ladyship. You will have saved the land.

CATHLEEN. Make no delay.

(He goes L.)

(ALEEL and OONA return)

CATHLEEN. They have not come; speak quickly.

ALEEL. One drew his knife And said that he would kill the man or woman That stopped his way; and when I would have stopped him He made this stroke at me; but it is nothing.

CATHLEEN. You shall be tended. From this day for ever I'll have no joy or sorrow of my own.

OONA. Their eyes shone like the eyes of birds of prey.

CATHLEEN. Come, follow me, for the earth burns my feet Till I have changed my house to such a refuge That the old and ailing, and all weak of heart, May escape from beak and claw; all, all, shall come Till the walls burst and the roof fall on us. From this day out I have nothing of my own.

(She goes.)

OONA (taking ALEEL by the arm and as she speaks bandaging his wound) She has found something now to put her hand to, And you and I are of no more account Than flies upon a window-pane in the winter.

(They go out.)

END OF SCENE 2.

SCENE 3

SCENE.—Hall in the house of COUNTESS CATHLEEN. At the Left an oratory with steps leading up to it. At the Right a tapestried wall, more or less repeating the form of the oratory, and a great chair with its back against the wall. In the Centre are two or more arches through which one can see dimly the trees of the garden. CATHLEEN is kneeling in front of the altar in the oratory; there is a hanging lighted lamp over the altar. ALEEL enters.

ALEEL. I have come to bid you leave this castle and fly Out of these woods.

CATHLEEN. What evil is there here? That is not everywhere from this to the sea?

ALEEL. They who have sent me walk invisible.

CATHLEEN. So it is true what I have heard men say, That you have seen and heard what others cannot.

ALEEL. I was asleep in my bed, and while I slept My dream became a fire; and in the fire One walked and he had birds about his head.

CATHLEEN. I have heard that one of the old gods walked so.

ALEEL. It may be that he is angelical; And, lady, he bids me call you from these woods. And you must bring but your old foster-mother, And some few serving men, and live in the hills, Among the sounds of music and the light Of waters, till the evil days are done. For here some terrible death is waiting you, Some unimagined evil, some great darkness That fable has not dreamt of, nor sun nor moon Scattered.

CATHLEEN. No, not angelical.

ALEEL. This house You are to leave with some old trusty man, And bid him shelter all that starve or wander While there is food and house room.

CATHLEEN. He bids me go Where none of mortal creatures but the swan Dabbles, and there 'you would pluck the harp, when the trees Had made a heavy shadow about our door, And talk among the rustling of the reeds, When night hunted the foolish sun away With stillness and pale tapers. No-no-no! I cannot. Although I weep, I do not weep Because that life would be most happy, and here I find no way, no end. Nor do I weep Because I had longed to look upon your face, But that a night of prayer has made me weary.

ALEEL (.prostrating himself before her) Let Him that made mankind, the angels and devils And death and plenty, mend what He has made, For when we labour in vain and eye still sees Heart breaks in vain.

CATHLEEN. How would that quiet end?

ALEEL. How but in healing?

CATHLEEN. You have seen my tears And I can see your hand shake on the floor.

ALEEL. (faltering) I thought but of healing. He was angelical.

CATHLEEN (turning away from him) No, not angelical, but of the old gods, Who wander about the world to waken the heart The passionate, proud heart—that all the angels, Leaving nine heavens empty, would rock to sleep.

(She goes to chapel door; ALEEL holds his clasped hands towards her for a moment hesitating, and then lets them fall beside him.)

CATHLEEN. Do not hold out to me beseeching hands. This heart shall never waken on earth. I have sworn, By her whose heart the seven sorrows have pierced, To pray before this altar until my heart Has grown to Heaven like a tree, and there Rustled its leaves, till Heaven has saved my people.

ALEEL. (who has risen) When one so great has spoken of love to one' So little as I, though to deny him love, What can he but hold out beseeching hands, Then let them fall beside him, knowing how greatly They have overdared?

(He goes towards the door of the hall. The COUNTESS CATHLEEN takes a few steps towards him.)

CATHLEEN. If the old tales are true, Queens have wed shepherds and kings beggar-maids; God's procreant waters flowing about

your mind Have made you more than kings or queens; and not you
But I am the empty pitcher.

ALEEL. Being silent, I have said all, yet let me stay beside you.

CATHLEEN.No, no, not while my heart is shaken. No, But you
shall hear wind cry and water cry, And curlews cry, and have the
peace I longed for.

ALEEL. Give me your hand to kiss.

```
CATHLEEN. I kiss your forehead.
And yet I send you from me. Do not speak;
There have been women that bid men to rob
Crowns from the Country-under-Wave or apples
        Upon a dragon-guarded hill, and all
That they might sift men's hearts and wills,
And trembled as they bid it, as I tremble
That lay a hard task on you, that you go,
And silently, and do not turn your head;
Goodbye; but do not turn your head and look;
Above all else, I would not have you look.
```

(ALEEL goes.)

I never spoke to him of his wounded hand, And now he is gone.

(She looks out.)

I cannot see him, for all is dark outside. Would my imagination
and my heart Were as little shaken as this holy flame!

(She goes slowly into the chapel. The two MERCHANTS enter.)
FIRST MERCHANT. Although I bid you rob her treasury, I find
you sitting drowsed and motionless, And yet you understand that
while it's full She'll bid against us and so bribe the poor That our
great Master'll lack his merchandise. You know that she has
brought into this house The old and ailing that are pinched the
most At such a time and so should be bought cheap. You've seen
us sitting in the house in the wood, While the snails crawled about

the window-pane And the mud floor, and not a soul to buy; Not even the wandering fool's nor one of those That when the world goes wrong must rave and talk, Until they are as thin as a cat's ear. But all that's nothing; you sit drowsing there With your back hooked, your chin upon your knees.

SECOND MERCHANT. How could I help it? For she prayed so hard I could not cross the threshold till her lover Had turned her thoughts to dream.

FIRST MERCHANT, Well, well, to labour. There is the treasury door and time runs on.

(SECOND MERCHANT goes Out. FIRST MERCHANT sits cross-legged against a pillar, yawns and stretches.)

FIRST MERCHANT. And so I must endure the weight of the world, Far from my Master and the revelry, That's lasted since— shaped as a worm—he bore The knowledgable pippin in his mouth To the first woman.

(SECOND MERCHANT returns with bags.)

Where are those dancers gone? They knew they were to carry it on their backs.

SECOND MERCHANT. I heard them breathing but a moment since, But now they are gone, being unsteadfast things.

FIRST MERCHANT. They knew their work. It seems that they imagine We'd do such wrong to our great Master's name As to bear burdens on our backs as men do. I'll call them, and who'll dare to disobey? Come, all you elemental populace From Cruachan and Finbar's ancient house. Come, break up the long dance under the hill, Or if you lie in the hollows of the sea, Leave lonely the long hoarding surges, leave The cymbals of the waves to clash alone, And shaking the sea-tangles from your hair Gather about us.

(The SPIRITS gather under the arches.)

26

SECOND MERCHANT. They come. Be still a while.

(SPIRITS dance and sing.)

FIRST SPIRIT. (singing) Our hearts are sore, but we come
Because we have heard you call.

SECOND SPIRIT. Sorrow has made me dumb.

FIRST SPIRIT. Her shepherds at nightfall Lay many a plate and
cup Down by the trodden brink, That when the dance break up We
may have meat and drink. Therefore our hearts are sore; And
though we have heard and come Our crying filled the shore.

SECOND SPIRIT. Sorrow has made me dumb.

FIRST MERCHANT. What lies in the waves should be indifferent
To good and evil, and yet it seems that these, Forgetful of their
pure, impartial sea, Take sides with her.

SECOND MERCHANT. Hush, hush, and still your feet. You are
not now upon Maeve's dancing-floor.

A SPIRIT. O, look what I have found, a string of pearls!

(They begin taking jewels out of bag.)

SECOND MERCHANT. You must not touch them, put them in
the bag, And now take up the bags upon your backs And carry
them to Shemus Rua's house On the wood's border.

SPIRITS. No, no, no, no!

FIRST SPIRIT. No, no, let us away; From this we shall not come
Cry out to' us who may.

SECOND SPIRIT. Sorrow has made me dumb.

(They go.)

SECOND MERCHANT. They're gone, for little do they care for me, And if I called they would but turn and mock, But you they dare not disobey.

FIRST MERCHANT (rising) These dancers Are always the most troublesome of spirits.

(He comes down the stage and stands facing the arches. He makes a gesture of command. The SPIRITS come back whimpering. They lift the bags and go out. Three speak as they are taking ub the bags.

FIRST SPIRIT. From this day out we'll never dance again.

SECOND SPIRIT. Never again.

THIRD SPIRIT. Sorrow has made me dumb.

SECOND MERCHANT (looking into chapel door) She has heard nothing; she has fallen asleep.

Our lord would be well pleased if we could win her. Now that the winds are heavy with our kind, Might we not kill her, and bear off her spirit Before the mob of angels were astir?

FIRST MERCHANT. If we would win this turquoise for our lord It must go dropping down of its free will But I've a plan.

SECOND MERCHANT. To take her soul to-night?

FIRST MERCHANT. Because I am of the ninth and mightiest hell Where are all kings, I have a plan.

(Voices.)

SECOND MERCHANT. Too late; For somebody is stirring in the house; the noise That the sea creatures made as they came hither,

Their singing and their endless chattering, Has waked the house. I hear the chairs pushed back, And many shuffling feet. All the old men and women She's gathered in the house are coming hither.

A VOICE. (within) It was here.

ANOTHER VOICE. No, farther away.

ANOTHER VOICE. It was in the western tower.

ANOTHER VOICE. Come quickly, we will search the western tower.

FIRST MERCHANT. We still have time—they search the distant rooms.

SECOND MERCHANT. Brother, I heard a sound in there—a sound That troubles me.

(Going to the door of the oratory and peering through it.) Upon the altar steps The Countess tosses, murmuring in her sleep A broken Paternoster.

FIRST MERCHANT. Do not fear, For when she has awaked the prayer will cease.

SECOND MERCHANT. What, would you wake her?

FIRST MERCHANT. I will speak with her, And mix with all her thoughts a thought to serve.— Lady, we've news that's crying out for speech.

(CATHLEEN wakes and comes to door of the chapel.)

Cathleen. Who calls?

FIRST MERCHANT. We have brought news.

CATHLEEN. What are you?

FIRST MERCHANT. We are merchants, and we know the book of the world Because we have walked upon its leaves; and there Have read of late matters that much concern you; And noticing the castle door stand open, Came in to find an ear.

CATHLEEN. The door stands open, That no one who is famished or afraid, Despair of help or of a welcome with it. But you have news, you say.

FIRST MERCHANT. We saw a man, Heavy with sickness in the bog of Allen, Whom you had bid buy cattle. Near Fair Head We saw your grain ships lying all becalmed In the dark night; and not less still than they, Burned all their mirrored lanthorns in the sea.

CATHLEEN.. My thanks to God, to Mary and the angels, That I have money in my treasury, And can buy grain from those who have stored it up To prosper on the hunger of the poor. But you've been far and know the signs of things, When will this yellow vapour no more hang And creep about the fields, and this great heat Vanish away, and grass show its green shoots?

FIRST MERCHANT. There is no sign of change—day copies day, Green things are dead—the cattle too are dead Or dying—and on all the vapour hangs, And fattens with disease and glows with heat. In you is all the hope of all the land.

CATHLEEN. And heard you of the demons who buy souls?

FIRST MERCHANT. There are some men who hold they have wolves' heads, And say their limbs—dried by the infinite flame— Have all the speed of storms; others, again, Say they are gross and little; while a few Will have it they seem much as mortals are, But tall and brown and travelled—like us—lady, Yet all agree a power is in their looks That makes men bow, and flings a casting-net About their souls, and that all men would go And barter those poor vapours, were it not You bribe them with the safety of your gold.

CATHLEEN. Praise be to God, to Mary, and the angels That I am wealthy! Wherefore do they sell?

FIRST MERCHANT. As we came in at the great door we saw Your porter sleeping in his niche—a soul Too little to be worth a hundred pence, And yet they buy it for a hundred crowns. But for a soul like yours, I heard them say, They would give five hundred thousand crowns and more.

CATHLEEN. How can a heap of crowns pay for a soul? Is the green grave so terrible a thing?

FIRST MERCHANT. Some sell because the money gleams, and some Because they are in terror of the grave, And some because their neighbours sold before, And some because there is a kind of joy In casting hope away, in losing joy, In ceasing all resistance, in at last Opening one's arms to the eternal flames.

In casting all sails out upon the wind; To this—full of the gaiety of the lost— Would all folk hurry if your gold were gone.

CATHLEEN. There is something, Merchant, in your voice That makes me fear. When you were telling how A man may lose his soul and lose his God Your eyes were lighted up, and when you told How my poor money serves the people, both— Merchants forgive me—seemed to smile.

FIRST MERCHANT. Man's sins Move us to laughter only; we have seen So many lands and seen so many men. How strange that all these people should be swung As on a lady's shoe-string,— under them The glowing leagues of never-ending flame.

CATHLEEN. There is a something in you that I fear; A something not of us; but were you not born In some most distant corner of the world?

(The SECOND MERCHANT, who has been listening at the door, comes forward, and as he comes a sound of voices and feet is heard.)

SECOND MERCHANT. Away now—they are in the passage—hurry, For they will know us, and freeze up our hearts With Ave Marys, and burn all our skin With holy water.

FIRST MERCHANT. Farewell; for we must ride Many a mile before the morning come; Our horses beat the ground impatiently.

(They go out. A number of PEASANTs enter by other door.)

FIRST PEASANT. Forgive us, lady, but we heard a noise.

SECOND PEASANT. We sat by the fireside telling vanities.

FIRST PEASANT. We heard a noise, but though we have searched the house We have found nobody.

CATHLEEN. You are too timid. For now you are safe from all the evil times. There is no evil that can find you here.

OONA (entering hurriedly) Ochone! Ochone! The treasure room is broken in, The door stands open, and the gold is gone.

(PEASANTS raise a lamentable cry.)

CATHLEEN. Be silent.

(The cry ceases.)

Have you seen nobody?

OONA Ochone! That my good mistress should lose all this money.

CATHLEEN. Let those among you—not too old to ride— Get horses and search all the country round, I'll give a farm to him who finds the thieves.

(A man with keys at his girdle has come in while she speaks. There is a general murmur of The Porter! the porter!")

PORTER. Demons were here. I sat beside the door In my stone niche, and two owls passed me by, Whispering with human voices.

OLD PEASANT. God forsakes us.

CATHLEEN. Old man, old man, He never closed a door Unless one opened. I am desolate, For a most sad resolve wakes in my heart But I have still my faith; therefore be silent For surely He does not forsake the world, But stands before it modelling in the clay And moulding there His image. Age by age The clay wars with His fingers and pleads hard For its old, heavy, dull and shapeless ease; But sometimes—though His hand is on it still— It moves awry and demon hordes are born.

(PEASANTS cross themselves.)

Yet leave me now, for I am desolate, I hear a whisper from beyond the thunder.

(She comes from the oratory door.)

Yet stay an instant. When we meet again I may have grown forgetful. Oona, take These two—the larder and the dairy keys.

(To the PORTER.)

But take you this. It opens the small room Of herbs for medicine, of hellebore, Of vervain, monkshood, plantain, and self-heal. The book of cures is on the upper shelf.

PORTER. Why do you do this, lady; did you see Your coffin in a dream?

CATHLEEN. Ah, no, not that. A sad resolve wakes in me. I have heard A sound of wailing in unnumbered hovels, And I must go down, down—I know not where— Pray for all men and women mad from famine; Pray, you good neighbours.

(The PEASANTS all kneel. COUNTESS CATHLEEN ascends the steps to the door of the oratory, and turning round stands there motionless for a little, and then cries in a loud voice:)

Mary, Queen of angels, And all you clouds on clouds of saints, farewell!

END OF SCENE 3.

SCENE 4

SCENE.—A wood near the Castle, as in Scene 2. The SPIRITS pass one by one carrying bags.

FIRST SPIRIT. I'll never dance another step, not one.

SECOND SPIRIT. Are all the thousand years of dancing done?

THIRD SPIRIT. How can we dance after so great a sorrow?

FOURTH SPIRIT. But how shall we remember it to-morrow?

FIFTH SPIRIT. To think of all the things that we forget.

SIXTH SPIRIT. That's why we groan and why our lids are wet.

(The SPIRITS go out. A group Of PEASANTS Pass.)

FIRST PEASANT. I have seen silver and copper, but not gold.

SECOND PEASANT. It's yellow and it shines.

FIRST PEASANT. It's beautiful. The most beautiful thing under the sun, That's what I've heard.

THIRD PEASANT. I have seen gold enough.

FOURTH PEASANT. I would not say that it's so beautiful.

FIRST PEASANT. But doesn't a gold piece glitter like the sun?
That's what my father, who'd seen better days, Told me when I was
but a little boy— So high—so high, it's shining like the sun, Round
and shining, that is what he said.

SECOND PEASANT. There's nothing in the world it cannot buy.

FIRST PEASANT. They've bags and bags of it.

(They go out. The two MERCHANTS follow silently.)

END OF SCENE 4

SCENE 5

SCENE.—The house of SHEMUS RUA. There is an alcove at the
back with curtains; in it a bed, and on the bed is the body of
MARY with candles round it. The two MERCHANTS while they
speak put a large book upon a table, arrange money, and so on.

FIRST MERCHANT. Thanks to that lie I told about her ships And
that about the herdsman lying sick, We shall be too much thronged
with souls to-morrow.

SECOND MERCHANT. What has she in her coffers now but
mice?

FIRST MERCHANT. When the night fell and I had shaped myself
Into the image of the man-headed owl, I hurried to the cliffs of
Donegal, And saw with all their canvas full of wind And rushing

35

through the parti-coloured sea Those ships that bring the woman grain and meal. They're but three days from us.

SECOND MERCHANT. When the dew rose I hurried in like feathers to the east, And saw nine hundred oxen driven through Meath With goads of iron, They're but three days from us.

FIRST MERCHANT. Three days for traffic.

(PEASANTS crowd in with TEIG and SHEMUS.)

SHEMUS. Come in, come in, you are welcome. That is my wife. She mocked at my great masters, And would not deal with them. Now there she is; She does not even know she was a fool, So great a fool she was.

TEIG. She would not eat One crumb of bread bought with our master's money, But lived on nettles, dock, and dandelion.

SHEMUS. There's nobody could put into her head

That Death is the worst thing can happen us. Though that sounds simple, for her tongue grew rank With all the lies that she had heard in chapel. Draw to the curtain.

(TEIG draws it.)

You'll not play the fool While these good gentlemen are there to save you.

SECOND MERCHANT. Since the drought came they drift about in a throng, Like autumn leaves blown by the dreary winds. Come, deal—come, deal.

FIRST MERCHANT. Who will come deal with us?

SHEMUS. They are out of spirit, Sir, with lack of food, Save four or five. Here, sir, is one of these; The others will gain courage in good time.

MIDDLE-AGED-MAN. I come to deal—if you give honest price.

FIRST MERCHANT (reading in a book) John Maher, a man of substance, with dull mind, And quiet senses and unventurous heart. The angels think him safe." Two hundred crowns, All for a soul, a little breath of wind.

THE MAN. I ask three hundred crowns. You have read there That no mere lapse of days can make me yours.

FIRST MERCHANT. There is something more writ here—"often at night He is wakeful from a dread of growing poor, And thereon wonders if there's any man That he could rob in safety."

A PEASANT. Who'd have thought it? And I was once alone with him at midnight.

ANOTHER PEASANT. I will not trust my mother after this.

FIRST MERCHANT. There is this crack in you—two hundred crowns.

A PEASANT. That's plenty for a rogue.

ANOTHER PEASANT. I'd give him nothing.

SHEMUS. You'll get no more—so take what's offered you.

(A general murmur, during which the MIDDLE-AGED-MAN takes money, and slips into background, where he sinks on to a seat.)

FIRST MERCHANT. Has no one got a better soul than that? If only for the credit of your parishes, Traffic with us.

A WOMAN. What will you give for mine?

FIRST MERCHANT (reading in book) "Soft, handsome, and still young "—not much, I think." It's certain that the man she's married to Knows nothing of what's hidden in the jar Between the hour-glass and the pepper-pot."

THE WOMAN. The scandalous book.

FIRST MERCHANT. "Nor how when he's away At the horse fair the hand that wrote what's hid Will tap three times upon the window-pane."

THE WOMAN. And if there is a letter, that is no reason Why I should have less money than the others.

FIRST MERCHANT. You're almost safe, I give you fifty crowns

(She turns to go.)

A hundred, then.

SHEMUS. Woman, have sense-come, Come. Is this a time to haggle at the price? There, take it up. There, there. That's right.

(She takes them and goes into the crowd.)

FIRST MERCHANT. Come, deal, deal, deal. It is but for charity We buy such souls at all; a thousand sins Made them our Master's long before we came.

(ALEEL enters.)

ALEEL. Here, take my soul, for I am tired of it. I do not ask a price.

SHEMUS. Not ask a price? How can you sell your soul without a price? I would not listen to his broken wits; His love for Countess

Cathleen has so crazed him He hardly understands what he is saying.

ALEEL. The trouble that has come on Countess Cathleen, The sorrow that is in her wasted face, The burden in her eyes, have broke my wits, And yet I know I'd have you take my soul.

FIRST MERCHANT. We cannot take your soul, for it is hers.

ALEEL. No, but you must. Seeing it cannot help her I have grown tired of it.

FIRST MERCHANT. Begone from me I may not touch it.

ALEEL. Is your power so small? And must I bear it with me all my days? May you be scorned and mocked!

FIRST MERCHANT. Drag him away. He troubles me.

(TEIG and SHEMUS lead ALEEL into the crowd.)

SECOND MERCHANT. His gaze has filled me, brother, With shaking and a dreadful fear.

FIRST MERCHANT. Lean forward And kiss the circlet where my Master's lips Were pressed upon it when he sent us hither; You shall have peace once more.

(SECOND MERCHANT kisses the gold circlet that is about the head of the FIRST MERCHANT.) I, too, grow weary, But there is something moving in my heart Whereby I know that what we seek the most Is drawing near—our labour will soon end. Come, deal, deal, deal, deal, deal; are you all dumb? What, will you keep me from our ancient home And from the eternal revelry?

SECOND MERCHANT. Deal, deal.

SHEMUS. They say you beat the woman down too low.

FIRST MERCHANT. I offer this great price: a-thousand crowns
For an old woman who was always ugly.

(An Old PEASANT WOMAN comes forward, and he takes up a book and reads.)

There is but little set down here against her. "She has stolen eggs and fowl when times were bad, But when the times grew better has confessed it; She never missed her chapel of a Sunday And when she could, paid dues." Take up your money.

OLD WOMAN. God bless you, Sir.

(She screams.)

Oh, sir, a pain went through me!

FIRST MERCHANT. That name is like a fire to all damned souls.

(Murmur among the PEASANTS, who shrink back from her as she goes out.)

A PEASANT. How she screamed out!

SECOND PEASANT. And maybe we shall scream so.

THIRD PEASANT. I tell you there is no such place as hell.

FIRST MERCHANT. Can such a trifle turn you from your profit? Come, deal; come, deal.

MIDDLE-AGED MAN. Master, I am afraid.

FIRST MERCHANT. I bought your soul, and there's no sense in fear Now the soul's gone.

MIDDLE-AGED MAN. Give me my soul again.

WOMAN (going on her knees and clinging to MERCHANT) And take this money too, and give me mine.

SECOND MERCHANT. Bear bastards, drink or follow some wild fancy; For sighs and cries are the soul's work, And you have none.

(Throws the woman off.)

PEASANT. Come, let's away.

ANOTHER PEASANT. Yes, yes.

ANOTHER PEASANT. Come quickly; if that woman had not screamed I would have lost my soul.

ANOTHER PEASANT. Come, come away.

(They turn to door, but are stopped by shouts of "Countess Cathleen! Countess Cathleen!")

CATHLEEN (entering) And so you trade once more?

FIRST MERCHANT. In spite of you. What brings you here, saint with the sapphire eyes?

CATHLEEN. I come to barter a soul for a great price.

SECOND MERCHANT. What matter, if the soul be worth the price?

CATHLEEN. The people starve, therefore the people go Thronging to you. I hear a cry come from them And it is in my ears by night and day, And I would have five hundred thousand crowns That I may feed them till the dearth go by.

FIRST MERCHANT.. It may be the soul's worth it.

CATHLEEN. There is more: The souls that you have bought must be set free.

FIRST MERCHANT. We know of but one soul that's worth the price.

CATHLEEN. Being my own it seems a priceless thing.

SECOND MERCHANT. You offer us—

CATHLEEN. I offer my own soul.

A PEASANT. Do not, do not, for souls the like of ours Are not precious to God as your soul is. O! what would Heaven do without you, lady?

ANOTHER PEASANT. Look how their claws clutch in their leathern gloves.

FIRST MERCHANT. Five hundred thousand crowns; we give the price. The gold is here; the souls even while you speak Have slipped out of our bond, because your face Has shed a light on them and filled their hearts. But you must sign, for we omit no form In buying a soul like yours.

SECOND MERCHANT. Sign with this quill. It was a feather growing on the cock That crowed when Peter dared deny his Master, And all who use it have great honour in Hell.

(CATHLEEN leans forward to sign.)

ALEEL (rushing forward and snatching the parchment from her) Leave all things to the builder of the heavens.

CATHLEEN. I have no thoughts; I hear a cry—a cry.

ALEEL (casting the parchment on the ground) I have seen a vision under a green hedge, A hedge of hips and haws-men yet shall hear

The Archangels rolling Satan's empty skull Over the mountaintops.

FIRST MERCHANT. Take him away.

(TEIG and SHEMUS drag him roughly away so that he falls upon the floor among the PEASANTS. CATHLEEN picks up parchment and signs, then turns towards the PEASANTS.)

CATHLEEN. Take up the money, and now come with me; When we are far from this polluted place I will give everybody money enough.

(She goes out, the PEASANTS crowding round her and kissing her dress. ALEEL and the two MERCHANTS are left alone.)

SECOND MERCHANT. We must away and wait until she dies, Sitting above her tower as two grey owls, Waiting as many years as may be, guarding Our precious jewel; waiting to seize her soul.

FIRST MERCHANT. We need but hover over her head in the air, For she has only minutes. When she signed Her heart began to break. Hush, hush, I hear The brazen door of Hell move on its hinges, And the eternal revelry float hither To hearten us.

SECOND MERCHANT. Leap feathered on the air And meet them with her soul caught in your claws.

(They rush Out. ALEEL crawls into the middle of the room. The twilight has fallen and gradually darkens as the scene goes on. There is a distant muttering of thunder and a sound of rising storm.)

ALEEL. The brazen door stands wide, and Balor comes Borne in his heavy car, and demons have lifted The age-weary eyelids from the eyes that of old Turned gods to stone; Barach, the traitor, comes And the lascivious race, Cailitin, That cast a druid weakness and decay Over Sualtem's and old Dectera's child; And that great king Hell first took hold upon When he killed Naisi and broke

Deirdre's heart, And all their heads are twisted to one side, For when they lived they warred on beauty and peace With obstinate, crafty, sidelong bitterness. (He moves about as though the air was full of spirits. OONA enters.)

Crouch down, old heron, out of the blind storm.

OONA. Where is the Countess Cathleen? All this day Her eyes were full of tears, and when for a moment Her hand was laid upon my hand it trembled, And now I do not know where she is gone.

ALEEL. Cathleen has chosen other friends than us, And they are rising through the hollow world. Demons are out, old heron.

OONA. God guard her soul.

ALEEL. She's bartered it away this very hour, As though we two were never in the world. And they are rising through the hollow world.

(He Points downward.)

```
First, Orchill, her pale, beautiful head alive,
Her body shadowy as vapour drifting
Under the dawn, for she who awoke desire
Has but a heart of blood when others die;
About her is a vapoury multitude
    Of women alluring devils with soft laughter
Behind her a host heat of the blood made sin,
But all the little pink-white nails have grown
To be great talons.
```

(He seizes OONA and drags her into the middle of the room and Points downward with vehement gestures. The wind roars.)

They begin a song And there is still some music on their tongues.

OONA (casting herself face downwards on the floor) O, Maker of all, protect her from the demons, And if a soul must need be lost, take mine.

(ALEEL kneels beside her, but does not seem to hear her words. The PEASANTS return. They carry the COUNTESS CATHLEEN and lay her upon the ground before OONA and ALEEL. She lies there as if dead.)

OONA. O, that so many pitchers of rough clay Should prosper and the porcelain break in two!

(She kisses the hands of CATHLEEN.)

A PEASANT. We were under the tree where the path turns, When she grew pale as death and fainted away. And while we bore her hither cloudy gusts Blackened the world and shook us on our feet Draw the great bolt, for no man has beheld So black, bitter, blinding, and sudden a storm.

(One who is near the door draws the bolt.)

CATHLEEN. O, hold me, and hold me tightly, for the storm Is dragging me away.

(OONA takes her in her arms. A WOMAN begins to wail.)

PEASANT. Hush!

PEASANTS. Hush!

PEASANT WOMEN Hush!

OTHER PEASANT WOMEN Hush!

CATHLEEN (half rising) Lay all the bags of money in a heap, And when I am gone, old Oona, share them out To every man and woman: judge, and give According to their needs.

A PEASANT WOMAN. And will she give Enough to keep my children through the dearth?

ANOTHER PEASANT WOMAN. O, Queen of Heaven, and all you blessed saints, Let us and ours be lost so she be shriven.

CATHLEEN. Bend down your faces, Oona and Aleel; I gaze upon them as the swallow gazes Upon the nest under the eave, before She wander the loud waters. Do not weep Too great a while, for there is many a candle On the High Altar though one fall. Aleel, Who sang about the dancers of the woods, That know not the hard burden of the world, Having but breath in their kind bodies, farewell And farewell, Oona, you who played with me, And bore me in your arms about the house When I was but a child and therefore happy, Therefore happy, even like those that dance. The storm is in my hair and I must go.

(She dies.)

OONA. Bring me the looking-glass.

(A WOMAN brings it to her out of the inner room. OONA holds it over the lips Of CATHLEEN. All is silent for a moment. And then she speaks in a half scream:)

O, she is dead!

A PEASANT. She was the great white lily of the world.

A PEASANT. She was more beautiful than the pale stars.

AN OLD PEASANT WOMAN. The little plant I love is broken in two.

(ALEEL takes looking-glass from OONA and flings it upon the floor so that it is broken in many pieces.)

ALEEL. I shatter you in fragments, for the face That brimmed you up with beauty is no more: And die, dull heart, for she whose mournful words Made you a living spirit has passed away And left you but a ball of passionate dust. And you, proud earth and plumy

46

sea, fade out! For you may hear no more her faltering feet, But are left lonely amid the clamorous war Of angels upon devils.

(He stands up; almost every one is kneeling, but it has grown so dark that only confused forms can be seen.)

And I who weep Call curses on you, Time and Fate and Change, And have no excellent hope but the great hour When you shall plunge headlong through bottomless space.

(A flash of lightning followed immediately by thunder.)

A PEASANT WOMAN. Pull him upon his knees before his curses Have plucked thunder and lightning on our heads.

ALEEL. Angels and devils clash in the middle air, And brazen swords clang upon brazen helms.

(A flash of lightning followed immediately by thunder.)

Yonder a bright spear, cast out of a sling, Has torn through Balor's eye, and the dark clans Fly screaming as they fled Moytura of old.

(Everything is lost in darkness.)

AN OLD MAN. The Almighty wrath at our great weakness and sin Has blotted out the world and we must die.

(The darkness is broken by a visionary light. The PEASANTS seem to be kneeling upon the rocky slope of a mountain, and vapour full of storm and ever-changing light is sweeping above them and behind them. Half in the light, haff in the shadow, stand armed angels. Their armour is old and worn, and their drawn swords dim and dinted. They stand as if upon the air in formation of battle and look downward with stern faces. The PEASANTS cast themselves on the ground.)

ALEEL. Look no more on the half-closed gates of Hell, But speak to me, whose mind is smitten of God, That it may be no more with mortal things, And tell of her who lies there.

(He seizes one of the angels.)

Till you speak You shall not drift into eternity.

THE ANGEL. The light beats down; the gates of pearl are wide. And she is passing to the floor of peace, And Mary of the seven times wounded heart Has kissed her lips, and the long blessed hair Has fallen on her face; The Light of Lights Looks always on the motive, not the deed, The Shadow of Shadows on the deed alone.

(ALEEL releases the ANGEL and kneels.)

OONA. Tell them who walk upon the floor of peace That I would die and go to her I love; The years like great black oxen tread the world, And God the herdsman goads them on behind, And I am broken by their passing feet.

(A sound of far-off horns seems to come from the heart of the Light. The vision melts away, and the forms of the kneeling PEASANTS appear faintly in the darkness.)

NOTES

I found the story of the Countess Cathleen in what professed to be a collection of Irish folk-lore in an Irish newspaper some years ago. I wrote to the compiler, asking about its source, but got no answer, but have since heard that it was translated from Les Matin`ees de Timoth`e Trimm a good many years ago, and has been drifting about the Irish press ever since. L`eo Lesp`es gives it as an Irish story, and though the editor of Folklore has kindly advertised for information, the only Christian variant I know of is a Donegal tale, given by Mr. Larminie in his West Irish Folk Tales and Romances, of a woman who goes to hell for ten years to save her husband, and stays there another ten, having been granted permission to carry away as many souls as could cling to her skirt.

L`eo Lesp`es may have added a few details, but I have no doubt of the essential antiquity of what seems to me the most impressive form of one of the supreme parables of the world. The parable came to the Greeks in the sacrifice of Alcestis, but her sacrifice was less overwhelming, less apparently irremediable. L`eo Lesp`es tells the story as follows:—

Ce que je vais vous dire est un r`ecit du car`eme Irlandais. Le boiteux, l'aveugle, le paralytique des rues de Dublin ou de Limerick, vous le diraient mieux que moi, cher lecteur, si vous alliez le leur demander, un sixpense d'argent `a la main.-Il n'est pas une jeune fille catholique `a laquelle on ne Fait appris pendant les jours de pr`eparation `a la communion sainte, pas un berger des bords de la Blackwater qui ne le puisse redire `a la veill`ee.

Il y a bien longtemps qu'il apparut tout-`a-coup dans la vielle Irlande deux marchands inconnus dont personne n'avait oui parler, et qui parlaient n`eanmoins avec la plus grande perfection la langue du pays. Leurs cheveux `etaient noirs et ferr`es avec de l'or et leurs robes d'une grande magnificence.

Tous deux semblaient avoir le m`eme age; ils paraissaient `etre des hommes de cinquante ans, car leur barbe grisormait un peu.

Or, `a cette `epoque, comme aujourd'hui, l'Irlande `etait pauvre, car le soleil avait `et`e rare, et des r`ecoltes presque nulles. Les indigents ne savaient `a quel sainte se vouer, et la mis`ere devenai de plus en plus terrible.

Dans l'h`otellerie o`u descendirent les marchands fastueux on chercha `a p`en`etrer leurs desseins: mais cc fut en vain, ils demeur`erent silencieux et discrets.

Et pendant qu'ils demeur`erent dans l'h`otellerie, ils ne cess`erent de compter et de recompter des sacs de pi`eces d'or, dont la vive clart`e s'apercevait `a travers les vitres du logis.

Gentlemen, leur dit l'h`otesse un jour, d'o`u vient que vous `etes si opulents, et que, venus pour secourir la mis`ere publique, vous ne fassiez pas de bonnes oeuvres?

-Belle h`otesse, r`epondit l'un d'eux, nous n'avons pas voulu aller au-devant d'infortunes honorables, dans la crainte d'`etre tromp`es par des mis`eres fictives: que la douleur frappe `a la porte, nous ouvrirons.

Le lendemain, quand on sut qu'il existait deux opulents `etrangers pr`ets `a prodiguer l'or, la foule assi`egea leur logis; mais les figures des gens qui en sortaient `etaient bien diverses. Les uns avaient la fiert`e dans le regard, les autres portaient la honte au front. Les deux trafiquants achetaient des `ames pour le d`emon. L'`ame d'un vieillard valait vingt pi`eces d'or, pas un penny de plus; car Satan avait eu le temps d'y former hypoth`eque. L'`ame d'une `pouse en valait cinquante quand elle `etait jolie, ou cent quand elle `etait laide. L'`Ame d'une jeune fille se payait des prix fous: les fleurs les plus belles et les plus pures sont les plus ch`eres.

Pendant ce temps, il existait dans la ville un ange de beaut`e, la comtesse Ketty O'Connor. Elle `etait l'idole du peuple, et la providence des indigents. D`es qu'elle eut appris que des m`ecr`eants profitaient de la mis`ere publique pour d`erober des coeurs `a Dieu, elle fit appeler son majordome.

—Master Patrick, lui dit elle, combien ai-je de pi`eces d'or dans mon coffre?

—Cent mille.

—Combien de bijoux?

—Pour autant d'argent.

—Combien de ch`ateaux, de bois et de terres?

—Pour le double de ces sommes.

—Eh bien! Patrick, vendez tout cc qui n'est pas or et apportez-m'en le montant. je ne veux garder `a moi que ce castel et le champs qui l'entoure.

Deux jours apr`es, les ordres de la pieuse Ketty `etaient ex`ecues et le tr`esor `etait distribu`e aux pauvres au fur et `a mesure de leurs besoins.

Ceci ne faisait pas le compte, dit la tradition, des commisvoyageurs du malin esprit, qui ne trouvaient plus d'`ames `a acheter.

Aides par un valet infame, ils p`en`etr`erent dans la retraite de la noble dame et lui d`erob`erent le reste de son tr`esor... en vain lutta-t-elle de toutes ses forces pour sauver le contenu de son coffre, les larrons diaboliques furent les plus forts. Si Ketty avait eu les moyens de faire un signe de croix, ajoute la l`egende Irlandaise, elle les eut mis en fuite, mais ses mains `etaient captives-Le larcin fut effectu`e.

Alors les pauvres sollicit`erent en vain pr`es de Ketty d`epouill`ee, elle ne pouvait plus secourir leur mis`ere;-elle les abandonnait `a la tentation. Pourtant il n'y avait plus que huit jours `a passer pour que les grains et les fourrages arrivassent en abondance des pays d'Orient. Mais, huit jours, c"etait un si`ecle: huit jours n`ecessitaient une somme immense pour subvenir aux exigences de la disette, et les pauvres allaient ou expirer dans les angoisses de la faim, ou, reniant les saintes maximes de l'Evangile, vendre `a vil prix leur `ame, le plus beau pr`esent de la munificence du Seigneur toutpuissant.

Et Ketty n'avait plus une obole, car elle avait abandonn`e son ch`ateaux aux malheureux.

Elle passa douze heures dans les larmes et le deuil, arrachant ses cheveux couleur de soleil et meurtrissant son sein couleur du lis: puis elle se leva r`esolue, anim`ee par un vif sentiment de d`esespoir.

Elle se rendit chez les marchands d'`ames.

—Que voulez-vous? dirent ils.

—Vous achetez des `ames?

—Oui, un peu malgr`e vous, n'est ce pas, sainte aux yeux de sapbir?

—Aujourd'hui je viens vous proposer un march`e, reprit elle.

—Lequel?

—J'ai une `ame `a vendre; mais elle est ch`ere.

—Qu'importe si elle est pr`ecieuse? L'`ame, comme le diamant, s'appr`ecie `a sa blancheur.

—C'est la mienne, dit Ketty.

Les deux envoy`es de Satan tressaillirent, Leurs griffes s'allong`erent sous leurs gants de cuir; leurs yeux gris `etincel`erent:—l'`ame, pure, immacul`ee, virginale de Ketty c'`etait une acquisition inappr`eciable.

—Gentille dame, combien voulez-vouz?

—Cent cinquante mille `ecus d'or.

—C'est fait, dirent les marchands: et ils tendirent `a Ketty un parchemin cachet`e de noir, qu'elle signa en frissonnant.

La somme lui fut compt`ee.

Des qu'elle fut rentr`ee, elle dit au majordome:

—Tenez, distribuez ceci. Avec la somme que je vous donne les pauvres attendront la huitaine n`ecessaire et pas une de leurs `ames ne sera livr`ee au d`emon.

Puis elle s'enferma et recommanda qu'on ne vint pas la d`eranger.

Trois jours se pass`erent; elle n'appela pas; elle ne sortit pas.

Quand on ouvrit sa porte, on la trouva raide et froide: elle `etait morte de douleur.

Mais la vente de cette `ame si adorable dans sa charit`e fut d`eclar`ee nulle par le Seigneur: car elle avait sauv`e ses concitoyens de la morte `eternelle.

Apr`es la huitaine, des vaisseaux nombreux amen`erent l'Irlande affam`ee d'immenses provisions de grains.

La famine n'`etait plus possible. Quant aux marchands, ils disparurent de leur h`otellerie, sans qu'on s`ut jamais ce qu'ils `etaient devenus.

Toutefois, les p`echeurs de la Blackwater pr`etendent qu'ils sont enchain`es dans une prison souterraine par ordre de Lucifer jusqu'au moment o`u ils pourront livrer l'`ame de Ketty qui leur a `echapp`e. je vous dis la l`egende telle que je la sais.

-Mais les pauvres l'ont racont`e d'`age en `age et les enfants de Cork et de Dublin chantent encore la ballade dont voici les derniers couplets:-

Pour sauver les pauvres qu'elle aime Ketty donna Son esprit, sa croyance m`eme Satan paya Cette `ame au d`evoument sublime, En `ecus d'or, Disons pour racheter son crime, Confiteor.

Mais l'ange qui se fit coupable Par charit`e

Au s`ejour d'amour ineffable Est remont`e. Satan vaincu n'eut pas de prise

Sur ce coeur d'or; Chantons sous la nef de l'`eglise, Confiteor.

N'est ce pas que ce r`ecit, n`e de l'imagination des po`etes catholiques de la verte Erin, est une V`eritable r`ecit de car`eme?

The Countess Cathleen was acted in Dublin in 1899, with Mr. Marcus St. John and Mr. Trevor Lowe as the First and Second Demon, Mr. Valentine Grace as Shemus Rua, Master Charles Sefton as Teig, Madame San Carola as Mary, Miss Florence Farr as Aleel, Miss Anna Mather as Oona, Mr. Charles Holmes as the Herdsman, Mr. Jack Wilcox as the Gardener, Mr. Walford as a Peasant, Miss Dorothy Paget as a Spirit, Miss M. Kelly as a Peasant Woman, Mr. T. E. Wilkinson as a Servant, and Miss May Whitty as The Countess Kathleen. They had to face a very vehement opposition stirred up by a politician and a newspaper, the one accusing me in a pamphlet, the other in long articles day after day, of blasphemy because of the language of the demons or of Shemus Rua, and because I made a woman sell her soul and yet escape damnation, and of a lack of patriotism because I made Irish men and women, who, it seems, never did such a thing, sell theirs. The politician or the newspaper persuaded some forty Catholic students to sign a protest against the play, and a Cardinal, who avowed that he had not read it, to make another, and both politician and newspaper made such obvious appeals to the audience to break the peace, that a score or so of police were sent to the theatre to see that they did not. I had, however, no reason to regret the result, for the stalls, containing almost all that was distinguished in Dublin, and a gallery of artisans alike insisted on the freedom of literature.

After the performance in 1899 I added the love scene between Aleel and the Countess, and in this new form the play was revived in New York by Miss Wycherley as well as being played a good deal in England and America by amateurs. Now at last I have made a complete revision to make it suitable for performance at the Abbey Theatre. The first two scenes are almost wholly new, and throughout the play I have added or left out such passages as a stage experience of some years showed me encumbered the action; the play in its first form having been written before I knew anything of the theatre. I have left the old end, however, in the version printed in the body of this book, because the change for dramatic purposes has been made for no better reason than that audiences—even at the Abbey Theatre—are almost ignorant of Irish mythology or because a shallow stage made the elaborate vision of armed angels upon a mountain-side impossible. The new end is particularly suited to the Abbey stage, where the stage platform can be brought out in front of the prosceniurn and have a flight of steps at one side up which the Angel comes, crossing towards the back of the stage at the opposite side. The principal lighting is from two arc lights in the balcony which throw their lights into the faces of the players, making footlights unnecessary. The room at Shemus Rua's house is suggested by a great grey curtain-a colour which becomes full of rich tints under the stream of light from the arcs. The two or more arches in the third scene permit the use of a gauze. The short front scene before the last is just long enough when played with incidental music to allow the scene set behind it to be changed. The play when played without interval in this way lasts a little over an hour.

The play was performed at the Abbey Theatre for the first time on December 14, 1911, Miss Maire O'Neill taking the part of the Countess, and the last scene from the going out of the Merchants was as follows:-

(MERCHANTS rush out. ALEEL crawls into the middle of the room; the twilight has fallen and gradually darkens as the scene goes on.)

ALEEL. They're rising up-they're rising through the earth, Fat Asmodel and giddy Belial, And all the fiends. Now they leap in the air. But why does Hell's gate creak so? Round and round, Hither and hither, to and fro they're running.

He moves about as though the air was full of spirits. OONA enters.)

Crouch down, old heron, out of the blind storm.

OONA. Where is the Countess Cathleen? All this day Her eyes were full of tears, and when for a moment Her hand was laid upon my hand, it trembled. And now I do not know where she is gone.

ALEEL. Cathleen has chosen other friends than us, And they are rising through the hollow world. Demons are out, old heron.

OONA. God guard her soul.

ALEEL. She's bartered it away this very hour, As though we two were never in the world.

(He kneels beside her, but does not seem to hear her words. The PEASANTS return. They carry the COUNTESS CATHLEEN and lay her upon the ground before OONA and ALEEL. She lies there as if dead.)

OONA. O, that so many pitchers of rough clay Should prosper and the porcelain break in two!

(She kisses the hands Of CATHLEEN.)

A PEASANT. We were under the tree where the path turns When she grew pale as death and fainted away.

CATHLEEN. O! hold me, and hold me tightly, for the storm is dragging me away.

(OONA takes her in her arms. A WOMAN begins to wail.)

PEASANTS. Hush!

PEASANTS Hush!

PEASANT WOMEN. Hush!

OTHER PEASANT WOMEN. Hush!

CATHLEEN. (half rising) Lay all the bags of money in a heap, And when I am gone, old Oona, share them out To every man and woman: judge, and give According to their needs.

A PEASANT WOMAN. And will she give Enough to keep my children through the dearth?

ANOTHER PEASANT WOMAN. O, Queen of Heaven, and all you blessed saints, Let us and ours be lost, so she be shriven.

CATHLEEN. Bend down your faces, Oona and Aleel; I gaze upon them as the swallow gazes Upon the nest under the eave, before She wander the loud waters. Do not weep Too great a while, for there is many a candle On the High Altar though one fall. Aleel, Who sang about the dancers of the woods, That know not the hard burden of the world, Having but breath in their kind bodies, farewell And farewell, Oona, you who played with me And bore me in your arms about the house When I was but a child-and therefore happy, Therefore happy even like those that dance. The storm is in my hair and I must go.

(She dies.)

OONA. Bring me the looking-glass.

(A WOMAN brings it to her out of inner room. OONA holds glass over the lips of CATHLEEN. All is Silent for a moment, then she speaks in a half-scream.)

O, she is dead!

A PEASANT. She was the great white lily of the world.

A PEASANT. She was more beautiful than the pale stars.

AN OLD PEASANT WOMAN. The little plant I loved is broken in two.

(ALEEL takes looking-glass from OONA and flings it upon floor, so that it is broken in many pieces.)

ALEEL. I shatter you in fragments, for the face That brimmed you up with beauty is no more; And die, dull heart, for you that were a mirror Are but a ball of passionate dust again! And level earth and plumy sea, rise up! And haughty sky, fall down!

A PEASANT WOMAN. Pull him upon his knees, His curses will pluck lightning on our heads.

ALEEL. Angels and devils clash in the middle air, And brazen swords clang upon brazen helms. Look, look, a spear has gone through Belial's eye!

(A winged ANGEL, carrying a torch and a sword, enters from the R. with eyes fixed upon some distant thing. The ANGEL is about to pass out to the L. when ALEEL speaks. The ANGEL Stops a moment and turns.)

Look no more on the half-closed gates of Hell, But speak to me whose mind is smitten of God, That it may be no more with mortal things: And tell of her who lies there.

(The ANGEL turns again and is about to go, but is seized by ALEEL.)

Till you speak You shall not drift into eternity. ANGEL. The light beats down; the gates of pearl are wide. And she is passing to the floor of peace, And Mary of the seven times wounded heart Has kissed her lips, and the long blessed hair Has fallen on her face; the Light of Lights Looks always on the motive, not the deed, The Shadow of Shadows on the deed alone.

(ALEEL releases the ANGEL and kneels.)

OONA. Tell them who walk upon the floor of peace.

That I would die and go to her I love, The years like great black oxen tread the world, And God the herdsman goads them on behind, And I am broken by their passing feet.

58

Made in the USA
Middletown, DE
18 January 2018